To all of my teachers who have
helped me along the way

Text and illustrations © 2010 by Gilbert Ford
All rights reserved. Published by Disney • Hyperion Books, an imprint
of Disney Book Group. No part of this book may be reproduced or
transmitted in any form or by any means, electronic or mechanical,
including photocopying, recording, or by any information storage and
retrieval system, without written permission from the publisher.
For information address Disney • Hyperion Books,
114 Fifth Avenue, New York, New York 10011-5690.
First Edition
10 9 8 7 6 5 4 3 2 1
F850-6835-5-09319
Printed in Singapore
Text set in Memphis
Reinforced binding
ISBN 978-1-4231-1997-5
Library of Congress Cataloging-in-Publication Data on file.
Visit www.hyperionbooksforchildren.com

flying lessons

GILBERT FORD

Disney • HYPERION BOOKS

New York

Every spring, when the air grew warm, the doves would fly north to enjoy their summer days. As they traveled, they would do everything in exactly the same way. To fly, they would raise their wings, then lower them, and then glide.

To pass the time, they would coo the same
tune until their beaks grew tired.

When they could no longer flap their wings,
the birds would rest on a wire above the highway.
There they would count the passing cars until
they fell asleep.

After finally arriving north, the doves
would settle into their separate trees.

They always passed their days the same way.

First they caught an early meal.

Then they took a dip in the bath.

And the rest of the day they sat, waiting for their eggs to hatch. This is the way that things were, and they saw no reason for a change.

One year, however, while they were traveling north, a strange bird joined them.

No one said anything, but something about
the newcomer really ruffled their feathers.

For one thing, he didn't seem
to have feathers. He was
covered in hard metal.

He was also much
larger than any bird
they had ever seen.

While most birds flapped their wings up,
then down, and glided . . .

this bird didn't move his wings at all.

When the doves tried to coo,
his loud hum drowned
out their music.

Resting along the highway was impossible.

The stranger made them so nervous
that they couldn't sleep.

When the flock arrived north, the outsider had difficulty finding his place among them.

He scared his
breakfast back
into its hole.

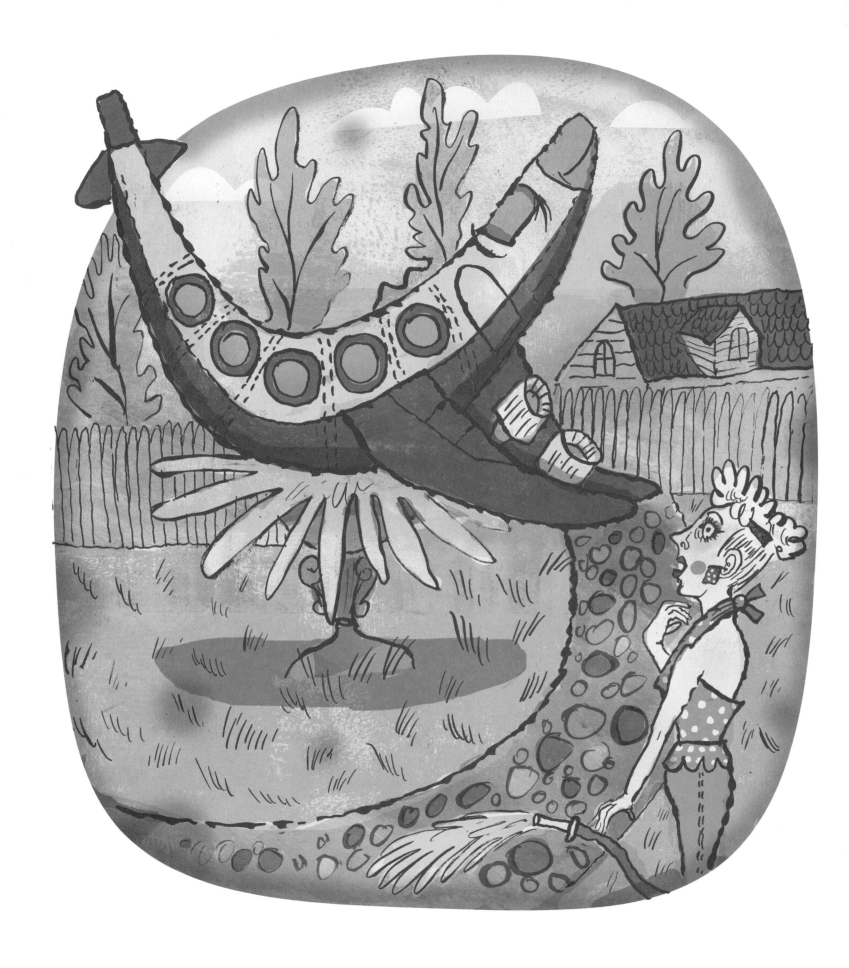

He made a splash in the birdbath.

And caring for eggs was completely out of the question.

Finally, the doves were fed up.
"You are not one of us," they squawked.
"Go fly with your own kind!"

The bizarre bird did not want to leave his friends,
but he could see there was no place for him.

The flock watched as his jet stream trailed across the sky.
Then they returned to their nests to sit over their eggs.

Later that summer, an early
arctic chill surprised the doves.

"What are we to do?!" they wondered.

"We cannot fly south now.

It's too cold."

Suddenly they heard a familiar loud
hum above them.

They looked up and saw the bizarre bird
making his way through the frosty sky.
Spotting his old friends below, he landed.

"Why are you sitting there shivering?" he asked.

"It is too cold to fly south," replied the doves. "We can barely move our wings."

"As you have pointed out, I cannot fly with you,"
replied the big bird. "But if you hop aboard,
then you can fly with me."

The big bird, who was actually a
passenger airplane, opened his door
to the doves and prepared for takeoff.

The birds cautiously boarded,
buckled their seat belts,
and took off into the sky.

As they journeyed through the clouds,
the doves saw things differently
than they had before.

That day, the plane did more than save
the doves' tail feathers from freezing;
he showed them a new way to fly.